Thornton W. Burgess
ANIMAL
TALES

Thornton W. Burgess
ANIMAL
TALES

Illustrations by Harrison Cady

Platt & Munk, Publishers · *New York*
A Division of Grosset & Dunlap

Stories in this compilation previously published individually and in a
single volume entitled *Animal Stories.*

Copyright © 1990 by Thornton W. Burgess Enterprises, Co.
Copyright © 1940, 1967 by Platt & Munk Co., Inc.
Published by Platt & Munk, Publishers,
a division of Grosset & Dunlap, Inc.,
which is a member of The Putnam Publishing Group, New York.
Library of Congress Catalog Card Number: 89-80884   ISBN 0-448-47286-4
A B C D E F G H I J

CONTENTS

ABOUT THE AUTHOR

Thornton W. Burgess, the respected storyteller, children's author, and naturalist, was born in Sandwich, Massachusetts in 1874. For more than half a century he devoted himself to writing about nature. His reverence for wildlife and concern for the environment led him to write more than 170 books about woodland animals to entertain and enlighten children all over the world.

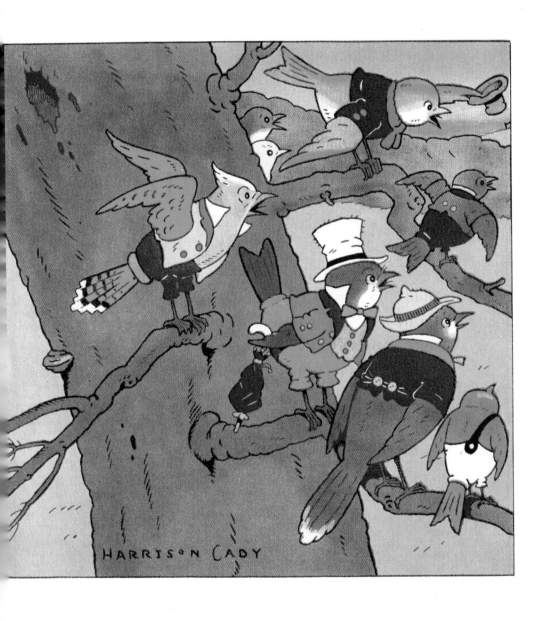

PETER RABBIT
PROVES
A FRIEND

Have thoughts for others if you would
Get all the joy from life you should.
—Peter Rabbit

It was spring. Peter Rabbit could hear and see and feel that this was true. He could hear birds singing, see green grass and swelling buds, and feel gentle Sister South Wind rumpling his fur.

Peter sat looking up the Crooked Little Path. Someone was coming. Yes, sir, someone was coming down the Crooked Little Path. It was Old Mr. Toad. Hop, hop, hippity-hop came Old Mr. Toad. He seemed to be in a hurry. Peter sat down squarely in Old Mr. Toad's way.

"Good day to you, Old Mr. Toad. You seem to be in a hurry," said Peter.

"I am," said Old Mr. Toad. "Don't stop me, Peter Rabbit. I'm late as it is. Don't you hear that chorus down in

the Smiling Pool? It needs my voice. I should have been
there days ago. Get out of my way, Peter, please."
Now it was a long way to the Smiling Pool and Peter

H CADY

did his best to persuade Old Mr. Toad that it wasn't safe for him to make the long journey. Peter said he would be much safer back in Farmer Brown's garden, where he belonged. But Old Mr. Toad insisted that he didn't belong there now. His place was down in the Smiling Pool, because in the spring he always met Mrs. Toad there and sang her his love song.

"I know she is waiting for me down there this very minute, so please get out of my way," said Old Mr. Toad.

Of course Peter did, but he shook his head doubtfully as he watched his homely old friend hurry on—hop, hop, hop, hop. Peter tried to decide whether he, too, would go down to the Smiling Pool or to the dear Old Briar Patch where he belonged. He did neither. Spring was in the

air and it got into Peter's heels. He raced with his own shadow and then tried to jump over it. He kicked his long heels in the air and did other foolish things just because it was spring. He couldn't sing, so he had to do something else to show how happy he felt.

Finally he was out of breath and had to sit down to rest. He happened to look down the Crooked Little Path. There was Old Mr. Toad coming back—hop, hop, hippity-hop—twice as fast as he had gone toward the Smiling Pool. He was pop-eyed. Yes, and he was trying to roll those pop eyes back to look behind him. He would have run right smack into Peter if Peter had not stepped aside.

"Hi there, Old Mr. Toad! You're not going in the right direction," cried Peter.

HARRISON CADY

"Yes I am. Yes I am, Peter Rabbit," gasped Old Mr.
Toad. "Yes I am." He stopped. He had to. He stopped to
get his breath. When he stopped he instantly faced
about and he looked more pop-eyed than ever. "Oh, dear!
Oh, dear me!" he cried. "I ought to be down in the Smil-

ng Pool this very minute and now I don't know when I ever will get there." There was a tear in each of his beauiful golden eyes.

"Tell me about it," said Peter. "Why are you coming back in such a hurry?"

"It isn't safe down there," said Old Mr. Toad in little more than a whisper. "No, sir, it isn't safe."

"Why isn't it safe?" asked Peter. He sat up hastily the better to see down the Crooked Little Path.

"Mr. Blacksnake is down there," replied Old Mr. Toad, and shook all over. "I saw him in the Crooked Little Path."

"Did he see you?" inquired Peter.

"I didn't wait to find out," replied Old Mr. Toad. "Oh dear! Oh, dear me! However shall I get to the Smiling Pool to sing?"

"I tell you what. I'll go ahead and, if I see Mr. Black-snake, I'll come back and let you know," said Peter.

Now one of Peter's hops is equal to a lot of Old Mr. Toad's hops. So in almost no time at all, Peter was so far

ahead that it was just as if Mr. Toad was alone. Old Mr. Toad stopped. He was in distress. Longing for the Smiling Pool was pulling him one way, and fear was pulling him the other way. He would hop a step forward and stop. Then fear would grip him and he would hop a step backward.

Meanwhile Peter Rabbit heedlessly scampered on. He forgot that Old Mr. Toad couldn't possibly keep up. Presently he came to an old leather strap that lay half hidden in the grass. He merely gave it a glance as he hopped over it. He had gone on several hops when a thought popped into his head. He stopped. He sat up. He looked back. Then he began to chuckle. "That was it!" exclaimed Peter. "As sure as I can hop that was it!"

"What was it?" a voice asked unexpectedly. There sat Johnny Chuck on his doorstep, a little to one side.

"Do you see Mr. Blacksnake over there?" Peter asked.

Johnny looked where Peter was pointing. "No," said he. "All I see is an old strap."

Peter chuckled again. "Old Mr. Toad didn't see an old strap. He saw Mr. Blacksnake and was frightened 'most to death," he said.

"Huh!" exclaimed Johnny Chuck. "Old Mr. Toad is always looking for Mr. Blacksnake and so he's always seeing him. Folks looking for trouble usually find it."

Peter hurried back. Old Mr. Toad was hopping forward, backward, forward, backward. "Is that a new kind of dance?" asked Peter.

"No," said Old Mr. Toad. "It isn't any kind of a dance. I'm just trying to go two ways at once and can't seem to go either way."

Peter's eyes twinkled. "Perhaps I can help you," he said. "That was nothing but an old black strap in the grass—not Mr. Blacksnake at all."

Old Mr. Toad sighed. It was a sigh of relief. "Peter," said he, "you are a friend indeed. Let's go!" Once more he was off for the Smiling Pool—hop, hop, hop, hop, hop.

REDDY FOX'S SUDDEN ENGAGEMENT

It always pays to be polite
To those with whom you dare not fight.
— Reddy Fox

There are all sorts of tails in the Green Forest—some handsome, some homely, some hardly worth calling tails. That of Reddy Fox is his footwarmer. That of Unc' Billy Possum is a sort of third hand with which to cling to branches when climbing. That of Peter Rabbit is a twinkling beacon in the dark. But Jimmy Skunk's tail is a signal, a warning signal, and the most respected tail in all the Green Forest.

Johnny Chuck had been bragging that there was no one his own size of whom he was afraid. Suddenly he met Jimmy Skunk. Johnny abruptly decided that he had business in the other direction. So he turned around and

started back up the Crooked Little Path. Do you know what Johnny wanted to do? He wanted to run. Yes, sir, that is what Johnny Chuck wanted to do. But his pride

wouldn't let him. So he tried to walk fast. But having short legs and being fat and heavy, he couldn't. Now Jimmy Skunk, who never liked to hurry, kept just a little way behind him without really trying.

It happened that Reddy Fox was hurrying down that Crooked Little Path, and right on a sharp turn he almost ran into Johnny Chuck. Jimmy Skunk was out of sight around the turn. He heard Reddy Fox exclaim and Johnny Chuck snarl. So Jimmy just stepped into the bushes where he couldn't be seen, but from which he could peep out and watch all that went on.

Johnny Chuck swelled up to look bigger than he really was. His hair stood on end to make him look still bigger.

He wished he had a rock to put his back against, for he knew that Reddy was much quicker than he and would try to get behind him. He wasn't afraid because there wasn't a cowardly hair on Johnny Chuck. He snarled and he growled and he showed his sharp teeth and dared Reddy Fox to come on.

Reddy made little rushes at Johnny Chuck and kept jumping from side to side. He hoped to get Johnny off his guard. Johnny had forgotten Jimmy Skunk, and Reddy didn't know Jimmy was in the neighborhood. Suddenly Jimmy stepped out beside Johnny Chuck. You should have seen Reddy Fox then. He stopped jumping about. He sat down at a little distance. He tried to grin.

"Hello, Jimmy Skunk," said Reddy. "I was just having a little fun with Johnny Chuck. We were just fooling, weren't we, Johnny?" Johnny merely growled.

"It's a nice day, Reddy," said Jimmy Skunk, moving forward and lifting his tail ever so little. It was a warning

that he was ready to use that scent that everyone dislikes so much.

"Isn't it," replied Reddy Fox, backing a little and never taking his eyes from that tail.

"I'm glad that you were just fooling and didn't mean

any harm to Johnny Chuck. I was afraid that you did," said Jimmy. He moved a few steps nearer and his tail rose a little higher.

"Oh, no! No indeed! Not for the world would I hurt Johnny Chuck!" exclaimed Reddy Fox. "Aren't you carrying your tail rather high, Jimmy Skunk," he added.

"Not in the presence of one who has such a handsome tail of his own," replied Jimmy politely. And he lifted his own tail almost straight up. "Were you on your way home, Reddy?"

"No," replied Reddy. "I was on my way to meet Mrs. Reddy."

"Then don't let us keep you. One should never be late for an appointment," said Jimmy, and moved forward slowly.

"Oh," replied Reddy Fox, "I won't be late. There is no hurry." Then he began to edge around behind Johnny Chuck, for he saw that Johnny seemed to have forgotten him. He was so busy watching Jimmy Skunk. Jimmy also saw this, and he knew just what Reddy was trying to do. But Jimmy pretended to notice nothing and gradually lowered his tail. Off a little way lay a piece of old bark. It reminded him of fat beetles. He was very fond of fat beetles. So he turned his back on Reddy Fox and walked over to that bark. He turned it over. Sure enough, under it were two fat beetles.

Now usually Jimmy Skunk moves slowly, and some people have the idea that he cannot move quickly. They haven't seen him catch fat beetles. In the wink of an eye, Jimmy had a black paw on each beetle.

Meanwhile Reddy Fox had managed to get a little be-

hind Johnny Chuck. Johnny was watching Jimmy catch those beetles and appeared to have forgotten Reddy. Reddy saw this and prepared to make a sudden jump on Johnny. What he didn't see was that Jimmy Skunk was watching him from the corner of his eye. Just as Reddy gathered his feet under him for a swift leap, Jimmy Skunk abruptly turned and ran straight toward Reddy Fox. Jimmy's tail was high over his back. For a second Reddy didn't move. Then, with a grin, he turned away. It was a sickly sort of grin.

"I'm sorry to have to leave such good company," he said, "but I've just remembered that Mrs. Reddy told me to be early. I find I will have to hurry so as not to keep her waiting. Good-by, Jimmy. Good-by, Johnny. I hope I will meet you both again soon. But not together," he added under his breath.

Then, pretending to be very dignified, he turned and went off up the Crooked Little Path. Jimmy looked at Johnny and grinned.

"Reddy's engagement was rather sudden, don't you think?" said he.

YOUNG FLASH THE DEER

Size and strength will often quit
Matched against a ready wit.
  —Old Mother Nature

Flash, handsome young son of Lightfoot the Deer, was now four months past his first birthday. He felt quite grown-up. Long ago the very last spot had disappeared from his coat.

"Only babies wear spotted coats," he scornfully told Jumper the Hare when Jumper admired the coats of Flash's small brother and sister.

He was no longer a fawn, and he wanted everybody to know it. Had not Mother, busy with the care of the twins,

sent him out to find a place for himself in the Great World? Best of all he had his first set of horns. My, my, how proud he was of them. All summer they had been growing. Flash

spent much time admiring them in his reflection in the still water of Paddy the Beaver's pond. At first they had been soft and tender. Now they were several inches long. On each was a small prong. And they were hard now, real weapons with which to fight anyone his own size. Yes, Flash felt quite grown-up.

Reddy Fox crossed his path. When Flash was younger he had feared Reddy. Now he snorted, lowered his head so as to present the sharp points of those horns, pawed the ground with a fore foot, and dashed at Reddy. Reddy merely leaped aside and grinned as Flash dashed past. When Flash turned, Reddy had disappeared in the bushes.

Head held high and white tail up, Flash proudly made his way to the pond of Paddy the Beaver. But he was too smart to allow pride to overcome caution. Before stepping out in the open, he carefully peered out from a place

where he could see all of Paddy's pond and the surrounding shore. There on the farther shore stood his father, Lightfoot the Deer. Flash was sure that nowhere else in all the Great World was a deer so handsome. His beautiful head was crowned with great antlers carrying ten points. It was held high. He looked startled yet unafraid as he started toward the end of Paddy's dam. Flash looked that way. There, standing upright like a man, was a great big Buster Bear. A little shiver of excitement ran all over Flash. What was going to happen?

He didn't have to wait long to find out. *Crack!* Over near the shore halfway between Lightfoot and Buster—and unseen by either—Paddy the Beaver had been floating. He had lifted that big broad tail of his as high as he could and brought it down on the water, *kerslap!* It made a report like a gun. Lightfoot leaped into the air, turned, and

with high bounds disappeared among the trees. Buster Bear dropped to all fours and lumbered off in the other direction. Flash whirled and bounded away. I suspect that Paddy the Beaver grinned, but of course I don't know.

In a few minutes Flash realized what had frightened him

so. He stopped running. He came to an old wood road. It led to an abandoned lumber camp. He remembered that over in that clearing he had found a big stump, around which he had found delicious salt. It had been put there for deer by fishermen who were camping in one of the

log buildings. They knew that deer travel miles and miles to find salt. It is the one thing they seem to crave most and never get enough of.

An old doe, Flash's grandma, had driven him away before he had time for more than a lick or two. Twice since, the same thing had happened. Perhaps today she wouldn't be there.

Flash stood just where the road left the woods. Grandma was there. There was bitter disappointment in his eyes. Beyond the old doe, his mother and the twins in their pretty spotted coats were quietly feeding. An idea popped into Flash's head. With a whistle as of alarm he bounded out into the clearing, running as only a badly frightened deer can run.

Grandma didn't wait to see what the danger might be. Away she bounded, her white flag, as a deer's tail is

called, straight up. Mother didn't stop to see what the danger might be. Off she bounded, her white flag up. At her heels bounded the twins, their little flags up, too. In a jiffy all had disappeared in the woods.

Flash stopped running. He walked over to the stump and began licking salt. Every few seconds he would lift his head to listen and to look over toward the woods where the others had vanished. By and by Grandma appeared. She was cautiously stealing back, looking for the cause of her fright and seeing if the way was now clear.

When she saw Flash at the salt, she forgot everything else. Hadn't she three times warned him to keep away from there? Out of the woods straight at Flash dashed Grandma. She reared high to strike him with her sharp-edged hoofs. Flash was watching and ready. He jumped aside and raced back up the old road. Grandma chased

him a little way, then returned and began feeding around the old stump. Mother and the twins did not return.

Flash kept out of sight up the road. After a while Grandma got over her nervousness. Mrs. Grouse came out from the woods and began to pick about near the big, old doe. They were old friends, those two. At last Grandma was facing straight away from where Flash was hiding. Her head was down as she nibbled grass. This was what Flash had been waiting for.

A crash in the brush back of them, and the sound of feet galloping as in fright, sent Mrs. Grouse whirring off in one direction and the big doe, leaping over logs and brush in headlong flight, in another direction to get out of sight among the trees.

Once more Flash had the salt to himself. This time Grandma did not return. When at last Flash was satisfied and started back to the pond of Paddy the Beaver for a drink, I fear he strutted a little. You know young people who do smart things sometimes do strut. They shouldn't but they do. And I think you will agree with me that Flash really had been smart to fool his wise old grandma.

PADDY'S SURPRISE VISITOR

*Some talents that we little guess
Our humblest neighbors may possess.*
    —Paddy the Beaver

Paddy the Beaver bit out the last chip from a tree he was cutting. The tree began to fall, ever so slowly. Paddy lifted his thick flat tail and brought it down hard on the ground. The sound of that slap could be heard for quite a distance. It was a signal, a warning to Mrs. Paddy, who was working near by. It meant for her to get out of the way of that falling tree. She ran. So did Paddy. The tree fell. At once they returned to it and began to trim off the limbs.

Paddy dragged a limb to the edge of the water. He was going to swim out with it to the food pile he and Mrs. Paddy were building near their house in the water. You know that in winter their food is the bark of the trees they have cut and stored in their food pile under water.

Paddy looked over to their house in the water. He
whistled. It was a low whistle, but it brought Mrs. Paddy
hurrying to his side.

"What is it?" she asked.

"Do you see what I see?" asked Paddy.

"Why—why someone is climbing up on the roof of our house!" she exclaimed. "Who do you suppose it can be?"

Now the eyes of Paddy and Mrs. Paddy were not as good as the eyes of some other little forest people. Their ears and their noses were better than their eyes. Not seeing him clearly, they took it for granted that their visitor was another beaver.

"I didn't know that there was another beaver anywhere about," said Paddy. "I wonder where that fellow came from."

Mrs. Paddy slid into the water. She headed straight for home. She didn't like the idea of a stranger prowling

around her home while she was absent. Paddy promptly followed.

"That fellow has a black coat for a beaver," thought Paddy as they drew near. "He is the blackest beaver I've ever seen."

Presently they stopped swimming to stare at the stranger on the roof. He wasn't a beaver. No sir, he wasn't a beaver. Who do you think he was? He was the last person in the world you would guess. He was Prickly Porky the Porcupine!

Paddy whistled in surprise. "Well!" he exclaimed. "Of all things! What are you doing on my house?"

"I'm resting, and if you don't like it you can go away," replied Prickly Porky crossly.

Paddy didn't know just what to say. He looked at the

thousand little spears in Prickly Porky's coat. Right then he knew that he didn't want any trouble with Prickly Porky.

"I didn't know you could swim," said Paddy, for the sake of saying something.

HARRISON CADY

"Well, you know it now. Why shouldn't I swim? Tell me hat," replied Prickly Porky rather peevishly.

"I don't know," admitted Paddy. "I just thought you ouldn't, that's all. I suppose you'll be telling us that you an dive and swim under water."

"I never tell things that aren't so. I can't dive and I can't swim under water. What is more, I don't want to do either," retorted Prickly Porky.

"Then I can't invite you into my house, for you see the door is under water," replied Paddy.

"The inside of your house doesn't interest me. The outside gives me a place to rest and that is all I care about," grunted Prickly Porky.

Mrs. Paddy gave a little sigh of relief. It was good to know that he couldn't dive or swim under water. "If he could and should," thought she, "we would just have to move out."

"Rest as long as you want to, Brother Porky," said Paddy, trying to be very polite. "Rest just as long as you want to."

Prickly Porky merely grunted and shook himself. Some of the little spears he carried in his coat fell out, but no

H. CADY

one noticed this. Finally he waddled down the roof into the water and headed for the shore. He was a funny sight. Yes, sir, he surely was. Paddy and Mrs. Paddy grinned. At the same time, they wondered how he could keep so high in the water. They didn't know that each of the thousand little spears in his coat—the things we call quills—were hollow and filled with air. He could hardly have helped floating so high.

Prickly Porky took his time. He paddled along slowly. He wasn't much of a swimmer, but he got there just the same. Paddy and Mrs. Paddy followed. Finally he approached the shore.

Now it just happened that Yowler the Bobcat had come down to the pond for a drink. He saw Prickly Porky coming and didn't recognize him, never having seen him in the water before.

"I don't know who that is, but it doesn't matter. I came here to get a drink, but now it looks as if I will get both a drink and a dinner," he thought. He crouched flat behind an old log. He licked his lips and his eyes gleamed with hunger and anticipation.

Prickly Porky waded ashore. He shook himself. The water flew from his coat and the thousand little quills rattled. Yowler, ready to spring, suddenly changed his mind. He snarled his disappointment. To have heard him you might have thought that he blamed Prickly Porky for being a porcupine. Then he turned and, with as much dignity as he could muster, walked away.

Slap! *Slap*! Two flat tails had hit the water hard. Paddy and Mrs. Paddy were expressing their pleasure in the disappointment of Yowler the Bobcat, whom they feared and hated. Then they swam back to their house and climbed on the roof.

"Ouch!" cried Paddy. He had stepped on one of Prickly Porky's quills.

"Ouch!" cried Mrs. Paddy. She had stepped on another.

THE
THREE
LITTLE
BEARS

Who silent keeps, with watchful eyes,
Is seldom taken by surprise.
                              —Sammy Jay

Someone had been into mischief. Someone had been meddling with the sap pails around Farmer Brown's sugar camp. Farmer Brown's boy meant to find out who that someone was. There was still snow in the Green Forest, and he had found footprints in it. Now he was following them. He didn't know it, but someone was following him. It was Sammy Jay. Sammy got a lot of fun from watching his neighbors. If you could get Sammy Jay to tell you all he knows about his neighbors, you would learn some surprising and interesting things.

Silently Sammy flew from tree to tree behind Farmer Brown's boy. There was no noisier tongue anywhere at

times than Sammy Jay's. But no one could be more
quiet than Sammy when he was spying on others. He was
chuckling inside. He knew whose footprints they were.

He knew who had meddled with those sap pails, drinking sap from some and knocking others from the trees where they had been hung. He wanted to be on hand when Farmer Brown's boy caught up with the maker of those footprints.

Farmer Brown's boy moved slowly. Carefully he put down each foot so as not to make a sound. He gently pushed aside branches that were in his way, taking care that not a single twig snapped. Soon he came to a big fallen tree. The tracks led around back of the upturned roots. Just as he started to follow them around, he came face to face with a young bear. Sammy Jay almost laughed aloud at the expressions on their faces. To this day he cannot tell which looked the most startled and surprised.

For a couple of seconds Farmer Brown's boy and the half-grown young bear stood absolutely still, staring at each other. The young bear recovered from his surprise first. He turned suddenly and started to run. Just to make him run faster Farmer Brown's boy yelled at him. At the sound of his voice there was a crash in the brush to one side of him, and a crash in the brush on the other side of him, and there were two more young bears trying to see which could run the fastest. Farmer Brown's boy yelled again. It was all so sudden and unexpected that for a moment he was as badly scared as the cubs.

But it was only for a minute or two. Then he began to laugh. He laughed and laughed. You see those little bears were frightened almost out of their wits. They did

what they had been taught they should do in time of danger—made straight for a tree—and all ran for the same tree. They tried to scramble up as fast as they had run, and in their haste they got in the way of each other. They tried to squeeze past each other and climb over

HARRISON CADY

each other, for each wanted to get to the highest branch. And all the time they were bawling, for they were three badly scared little bears.

Such a funny sight they were! Farmer Brown's boy laughed and laughed. Then his laugh was suddenly cut

off. He almost swallowed it. With no warning at all there came a deep, loud, ugly-sounding *woof, woof, woof!* Out of the thicket rushed a big bear with the wickedest looking eyes, and the most awful teeth, and the most dreadful sounding voice. It was Mother Bear, and to Farmer Brown's boy she looked as big as an elephant.

He didn't move. He couldn't. He was too scared. His eyes seemed to be popping right out of his head. He didn't yell again because he couldn't. Straight at Farmer Brown's boy rushed Mother Bear, snapping her jaws and making a terrible noise. Just a few feet from him she stopped. She glared at him. He stared at her. Sammy Jay, looking on, held his breath. What was going to happen? Even

the three little bears stopped whimpering. Clinging to the top of the tree they were looking down in round-eyed excitement.

For two long minutes Mother Bear and Farmer Brown's boy faced each other, neither moving. Farmer Brown's boy knew that if he should turn to run, Mother Bear would know that he was afraid and would be on his back before he could take more than a few steps. Still growling a rumbly, grumbly growl deep down in her throat, Mother Bear turned her head and looked up at the little bears. She took a couple of steps toward that tree, then looked back to growl at Farmer Brown's boy. He didn't move. He just stared at her.

HARRISON CADY

Turning every few steps to growl a dreadful threat, Mother Bear slowly retreated to the foot of the tree in which were her three cubs. Happy to be near their mother again, the little bears began to scramble down. They were in such a hurry that they didn't stop to climb all the way down, but when still some distance from the ground let go and dropped. *Thump, thump, thump* they landed, and crowded close to Mother Bear.

Slowly Farmer Brown's boy backed away. As soon as he dared, he walked quickly. Then he ran. Trying to look behind, instead of watching his steps, he tripped and fell. He scrambled to his feet and continued to run.

"Phew!" he exclaimed when he was sure he was not being followed. "Phew! I never was so scared in all my life! I bluffed that old bear into thinking I wasn't afraid, but I was just the same."

And the funny part is that Mother Bear was chuckling down inside as she thought of how she had bluffed Farmer Brown's boy. You see, she had no intention of attacking him. She was only pretending.

A ROBBER
MEETS
HIS MATCH

Already he has won a fight
Who knows his cause is just and right.
—Happy Jack Squirrel

Robber the Rat had recently come to live in a hole under the old stone wall. He was sitting at the entrance now, watching Happy Jack the Gray Squirrel and his family at their breakfast table. This was a big flat stone on the top of the wall. Every morning Farmer Brown's boy spread a breakfast there for the squirrels. And every morning since he had come over there to live, Robber had driven the squirrels away and stolen all the food for himself just as soon as Farmer Brown's boy went away.

Now as Robber watched those squirrels he noticed that they did not appear to be hungry. Instead of eating they

had their heads together and seemed to be talking.

"I wonder what they are up to now," thought Robber.

As if in answer Mrs. Happy Jack and the four half-

grown children left the old wall and climbed up in the nearest tree. Happy Jack remained and settled down to enjoy his breakfast. It was a good breakfast. He smacked his lips. Robber heard it and gritted his teeth.

"Only one to fight this morning. I'll make that fellow take to his heels in short order," he muttered, and with a savage rush he leaped up on that breakfast table.

Then Robber received one of the greatest surprises of his life. Instead of turning tail and running, Happy Jack sprang to meet him. There was nothing of the coward in the appearance of Happy Jack. The glare in his eyes was quite as fierce as the glare in the eyes of Robber the Rat.

Biff! They met with jaws snapping and hind feet kicking and ripping. My, oh my, such a fight as that was! Robber was a notorious fighter. He had often been heard

to say that he would rather fight than eat. He had no
fear of Happy Jack. In fact, he always thought of Happy
Jack as rather a coward. Hadn't he more than once seen
little Chatterer the Red Squirrel chase his big gray cousin
all through the Old Orchard? What he didn't know was
that Happy Jack ran to try to escape annoyance—not
from fear.

Such a fight as that was while it lasted! There was
kicking and biting and scratching! The fur flew! There
was growling! There was squealing! Over and over, locked
together, rolled Happy Jack and Robber the Rat. They fell
off the wall to the ground, but this did not separate
them.

All the feathered folk in the Old Orchard hurried over
to look on and chatter and scream excitedly. Sammy
Jay, Bully the English Sparrow, Scrapper the Kingbird,

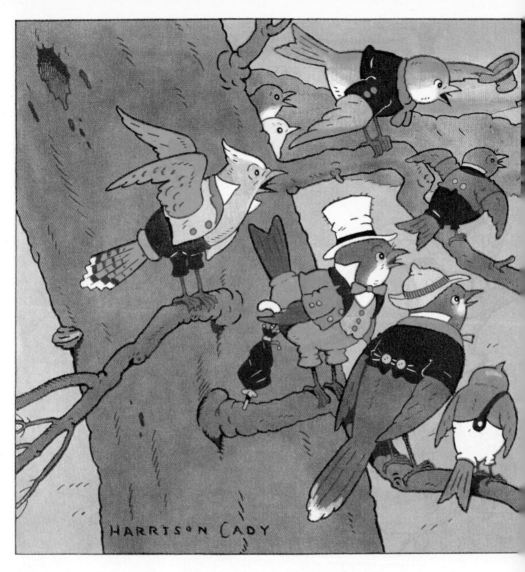

HARRISON CADY

Welcome Robin, Winsome Bluebird, Tommy Tit the
Chickadee, Jenny Wren, Goldie the Oriole, Skimmer the
Swallow—all were there. While some of them had often
quarreled with Happy Jack, all were for him now. Except
among his own kind, Robber the Rat hadn't a friend in

the world. He was an outlaw and an outcast. Striped
Chipmunk danced up and down at a safe distance on the
old wall, and Chatterer the Red Squirrel came racing
over from the Green Forest.

Robber fought savagely. He hadn't been in the least

afraid of Happy Jack. Why, more than once he had put
to flight a cat more than twice his own size. So imagine
how surprised he was when he found that he was getting
more than he had bargained for. It was hard to admit
that he was getting the worst of that fight, but facts are
facts. After a while Robber realized that if he wanted to
save his life he must get away from Happy Jack.

This was easier thought of than done, but at last Happy
Jack lost his grip for just a second and with a sudden
wrench Robber tore loose. Then he wasted no time. He
started for his hole as fast as his somewhat wobbly legs
would take him. He was a sorry sight. His coat was torn
and he was covered with bites and scratches. Fear gave
him strength, for right at his heels was Happy Jack
making a most unpleasant sound by snapping his teeth
together.

Into his hole under the old wall plunged Robber. Happy Jack stopped at the entrance. He didn't like the idea of going down in the ground. So he sat outside and made dreadful threats and dared Robber to come out again. Robber did nothing of the kind. So at last Happy Jack marched triumphantly back to the breakfast which had been so rudely interrupted. Mrs. Squirrel and the four children came down to join him. How their tongues flew as they talked it all over! How they praised Happy Jack! How proud they were of him! Every now and then Happy Jack would jump down and run over to Robber's hole and dare him to come out.

All the other folk in the Old Orchard said nice things about Happy Jack. He had won their respect and they told him so. None had ever seen him fight like that before and they were proud of him.

"It was nothing," said Happy Jack modestly. "One who will not fight for his rights deserves to lose them. I guess that fellow won't try to rob any of us again in a hurry."

That was a very good guess, for that night when the

Black Shadows had crept out from the Purple Hills and wrapped the Old Orchard in darkness, Robber crept up to the entrance to his hole and peeped out. Happy Jack and the other folk had gone to bed. Robber came out. Hurriedly he sneaked across the barnyard, to the big barn where he had made his home before he had ventured over to that hole under the old wall.

"I didn't know a squirrel's teeth are so sharp," he kept saying over and over as he hurried along.

But even that experience didn't lead Robber the Rat to mend his ways. He is still an outlaw and an outcast wherever he may be.

HCADY

BOBBY COON'S MISTAKE

You'll find beyond the smallest doubt
Mistakes are bound to be found out.
                    —Bobby Coon

H. CADY

Bobby Coon, he of the ringed tail and black mask, is just like everybody else—he makes mistakes. Everybody does, grown-ups as well as boys and girls. It is through mistakes that many important lessons are learned.

Bobby sat in the doorway of his hollow tree, looking out. He had just awakened from a long sleep. He is one of those whom the Indians call the Seven Sleepers. These are the furry folk who, snug and comfortable in their homes, sleep through the coldest part of the winter. The biggest is Buster Bear, and the smallest is little Nimble-

heels the Jumping Mouse. The others are Striped Chipmunk, Jimmy Skunk, Johnny Chuck and Flitter the Bat.

Bobby yawned. Then he climbed down to the ground.

First he stretched one hind leg. Then he stretched the other hind leg. Finally he stretched both front legs together.

"Woof, woof!" said a deep rumbly-grumbly voice just back of him.

Bobby Coon was so startled that in his haste to get away he turned a complete somersault. You see he was a little stiff and clumsy from his long winter sleep. He was hardly awake yet. He scrambled to his feet and raced away, trying to look behind himself instead of watching where he was going. He didn't realize that he was near the Laughing Brook until he went over the edge of the bank. He was right at the top of Little Joe Otter's slippery slide. Out from under him flew Bobby's feet! Down he slid on his back, his legs kicking wildly. *Splash!* The water flew. Bobby gasped. He shook his head. Then he began to swim for a place where the bank was low. My, that water was

cold. He couldn't get out of it quickly enough. There was no leftover sleepiness in him now. Not a bit. He was wide awake.

"Caw, caw, ca-a-aw, caw!" shrieked Blacky the Crow from the top of a tree from which he had seen the whole performance. "Do it again, Bobby! Do it again!"

"Go on, do it again," said the same deep rumbly-grumbly voice that had so startled him in the first place, and grinning broadly Buster Bear stepped out from behind a tree.

Bobby Coon said nothing at all. He stopped only long enough to shake himself, sending the water flying in all directions. Then he took to his heels and this time he didn't try to look behind. He wanted to get out of sight and back to his hollow tree as soon as possible. Buster Bear was a sort of big cousin of the Coon family, but Bobby Coon had no cousinly feeling just then.

The next morning he was out again for a bit of exercise.
He was also out again that night, for he was beginning to
grow hungry. Day and night he was roaming about, for
all the time he was growing thinner and hungrier. Food
was scarce as yet and hard to find. He had used up the fat

stored under his skin in the fall. That is why he grew thinner and thinner, and ran about more and more.

One morning he was near where Blacky the Crow and Mrs. Blacky had had their nest the year before.

"I wonder if the Blackys are using that nest again this

year," he muttered. "I suppose it is a bit early for that yet, but it will do no harm to look. I've known them to nest as early as this. If there should happen to be eggs in that nest—" Bobby didn't finish. Instead he licked his lips.

He shuffled over to the tree in which the nest was. He looked up at it. Then he looked in the tops of neighboring trees. The crows were nowhere to be seen.

"It is just as well they are not around," muttered Bobby. "I'll just have a look while they are away."

He began to climb the tree. Halfway up he stopped for a moment. It was then that he thought he heard a faint sound above him. He pricked up his ears to listen. There it was again.

"If I didn't know that it is too early, I would think that there are young crows up in that nest. Yes, sir, I would indeed. But there are no young birds of any kind so

early in the season as this. I wish there were," he thought.

That was a mistake, as he was to find out shortly. A merry little breeze came down from the treetop and tickled his nose with the smell of meat. He sniffed. Then he made another mistake. He didn't stop to wonder how it could be that meat was up in the top of the tree. He began to scramble up as fast as he could, not even looking around to see if there was anyone about. That was a third mistake.

He was almost to the nest. He was sure now that the meat smell came from that nest. His mouth watered. Then, without warning, he was given one of the greatest and most unpleasant surprises of his whole life. He had seen no one and heard no one when he received a terrible blow.

He lost his grip and fell, but he didn't fall far. He caught hold of a limb and hung on. Bobby was very

much at home in trees. He didn't know who or what had
hit him. But he soon found out. Hardly had he pulled
himself up on the limb when a great bird, with the
fiercest yellow eyes, swooped down and struck him. It
was Hooty the Great Horned Owl.

This time Bobby held on. He snarled as he climbed around to the other side of the tree. That blow had hurt. He knew now why he hadn't seen Blacky the Crow or Mrs. Blacky. The big owls had taken their nest. It must be that they had young in there already and the meat he had smelled had been left there for them to eat. What a mistake he had made! What a dreadful mistake! He quickly started to scramble down.

Biff! It was *Mrs.* Hooty Owl who hit him this time. He fell. He bounced from limb to limb. He hit the ground with a thump. It knocked the breath from him, but he didn't wait to get it back. He was on his feet and running before you could wink. He had lost his appetite, but had learned a lesson he never would forget as long as he lived—never to take a thing for granted.

THE END